For Jack, Megan, and Ella

First U.S. edition 2017

Library of Congress Catalog Card Number pending
ISBN 978-0-7636-9648-1

17 18 19 20 21 22 TLF 10 9 8 7 6 5 4 3 2 1

Printed in Dongguan, Guangdong, China

This book was typeset in ITC Highlander Book, Slappy Inline, and Goudy Old Style.
The illustrations were done in crayon, acrylic, and watercolor and completed digitally.

TEMPLAR BOOKS

an imprint of
Candlewick Press
99 Dover Street
Somerville, Massachusetts 02144
www.candlewick.com

The Fox and the Wild

Clive McFarland

templar books
an imprint of Candlewick Press

This is **Fred.**

He lived in the
middle of a **big** city.

But the city was smoky,

noisy,

and very, very fast.

Fred's cousins **loved** living in the city,
especially at night, when the streets were quiet.

"Let's raid the garbage," said
Fred's cousin.

"That sounds dangerous,"
said Fred.

"It sounds exciting!"
said his other cousin.

So Fred kept watch while his
cousins made a nighttime raid.
Then . . .

CRASH!

BANG!

"Get out of there!" yelled an angry voice.

The foxes fled. Fred's cousins went one way . . .

and Fred went another.

Fred climbed onto a
rooftop to hide.

Above him, he saw a flock of birds flying over the city.

"Where are you going?" Fred called.

But his voice was carried off by the wind.

Fred had to find
out where they
were going.

"Where do the birds go?" he asked a tired dog.
"I've never really thought about it," said the dog.

"Have you ever followed the birds?" he asked a skinny cat.
"They get away," said the cat.

"Do they fly beyond the city?" he asked a watchful rat.
"There's no such place," said the rat.

Fred wasn't convinced. The city couldn't go on forever.

Suddenly
something
came
tumbling
out of
the sky.

"Honk!"

It was one
of the birds.

"Please don't eat me!" cried the bird.

"I don't want to," said Fred. "I just want to know where the birds go."

"We go to the wild," said the bird. "Where the trees spread their branches and the wind blows over the hills. That's where I was going."

And then the bird flew off.

Fred knew he needed to see the wild for himself.
The bird said there are trees in the wild, he remembered.

But this place didn't seem like the wild.

The wild wouldn't be so bare, thought Fred.
And the bird said the wind blows in the wild. . . .

But this place didn't seem like the wild, either.

The air is too dirty here, Fred thought, coughing.
The bird said there were hills in the wild. . . .

But this place didn't seem like the wild.
The ground is too hard here, thought Fred.

He didn't know where to go next.

Just then . . .

SCREECH!
CRUNCH!

Fred ran for cover.

He was in a
tunnel, where it
was too dark
to see.

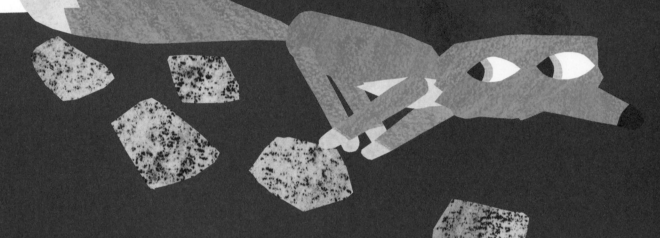

Fred tried not
to be scared.

Finally he tumbled out
the end and into . . .

a place with **trees.**

Real **wild** trees. They were greener
than anything he'd ever seen.

And the ground was
softer than anything
he'd ever walked on.

A wild breeze swept around Fred.

He'd never smelled anything so wonderful.

Fred heard animals scurrying in the undergrowth.
They sounded better than anything he'd ever heard.

Fred took a breath
of **clean,**
wild air,

and **ran** over the **hills.**

He had found it.

"I'm in the WILD!"
he barked.

"Hello," said a voice.

"Do you know where
the birds go?"